A Cowboy in the Woods
A Junior Game Warden Book

Copyright © Wayne Saunders 2021

ISBN: 978-1-7349308-9-4

731 Tasker Hill Rd.
Conway, NH 03818
USA
www.tmcbooks.com

Junior Game Warden Series:

A Cowboy In the Woods

By Wayne Saunders and Lindsay Webb

Bobby Forest is eight years old and loves to explore outdoors. He likes to wear his fishing vest because it has so many pockets. In his vest he has a magnifying glass, a tiny notebook and a pencil he "borrowed" from the mini-golf place, a whistle, a pocketknife, three plastic dinosaurs, and five quartzite rocks.

2

While walking down the road, on his usual route around the neighborhood exploring and observing nature, Bobby finds the victim of an unfortunate accident, a dead frog. Bobby walks around and observes the dead frog from many angles. He pulls out his magnifying glass and peers very closely at the frog and writes in his notebook:

Beep Beep! A car slows down and goes by Bobby It's Mr. Peters from nex door.

"What are you doing down there, Bob-by? You're gonna get run over playing in the road." Bobby waves to Mr. Peters and mumbles, "Sorry."

"Aha!" Bobby thinks, "My first suspect in the case! Mr. Peters and his car!"

Bobby starts working on his interview questions, but first asks his little brother Jeremy if he'd like to be the coroner and his little sister, Kate, the funeral director. They get right to work.

After school the next day, Bobby gets right to work on his frog case. First he checks in with his brother and sister. Jeremy reports that the cause of death was "being squished." Bobby adds this to his notebook. Kate informs the entire family that there will be a funeral that evening after dinner and that everyone is expected to say a few words for the dear departed Mr. Froggy.

Bobby walks next door and knocks on Mr. Peters' door. The door opens up and Bobby asks, "Where were you between 9 am and 3 pm on Tuesday?" His pencil is ready to write down the confession.

"Hello, Bobby. What is this, an interrogation?" Mr. Peters asks, peering down from his glasses.

"Just answer the question, Mr. Peters, or I'll have to bring you down to the station," Bobby says.

"Well, ah, okay. On Tuesday, hmmm....I was home all day until 3:15."

"Until 3:15? Are you sure?" Bobby asks.

"Yes, I went out at 3:15 to go to the post office and then I drove home. Isn't that when I saw you playing in the road?" asked Mr. Peters with a raised eyebrow.

"Hmmm.....yes," Bobby answers quietly.

"What's this all about anyway?" asks Mr. Peters.

"My case. A frog, Mr. Froggy, was squished."

"Oh, I'm so sorry. I'm afraid that you won't be able to tell whose car did it though, unless you interview everyone who drove down the road that day. And even then, they might not confess. But keep your chin up, Bobby. Some crimes go un- solved for years until you can figure them out. Wait, I've got something for you."

Mr. Peters goes back inside and comes back out with binoculars.

"I was cleaning out my old backpack the other day and found these binoculars. Since you are doing a lot of investigating, maybe you could use them?"

Bobby takes the binoculars from Mr. Peters' hands and holds them up to his eyes. They are fuzzy and a little scratched, but Mr. Peters shows him how to adjust them and soon he can spy a bird's nest in a tree at the edge of the yard. These will come in very handy!

"Thanks, Mr. Peters," Bobby calls as he races down the walkway. It's almost dinner time and he still has to write Mr. Froggy's eulogy.

12

That weekend, Bobby's Dad suggests that the two of them go fishing. Still feeling a little dejected about not solving the frog case, Bobby thinks that getting back into the game is a good idea and slips on his fishing vest, which weighs a little more with his new binoculars.

Bobby's Dad is a really good fisherman and is really good at reading clues in the woods. His Dad often shows him clues left behind from wildlife: deer scat (or poop), a black bear hair stuck on some tree bark, and even how to tell that a snowshoe hare has eaten a twig. Sometimes Bobby understands and sees the clues, but other times it's harder to see them. His Dad says that he just has to keep practicing and he'll be able to read the clues too.

Bobby lets his Dad cast into the pond first, watching how his wrist flicks just so while his fingers let go of the line. Bobby mimics the movement with his own rod and smiles proudly at his cast.

"Looking pretty good there, Bobby." His Dad seems impressed.

They hear a sudden rustling noise, and out of nowhere a man pops out of the woods. The man is tall and wears dark green with patches on the sleeves. His belt is filled with gadgets. Bobby recognizes a cell phone and a gun, but the other things on his belt are a mystery. As the man approaches Bobby and his Dad, his hand reaches up to the brim of a cowboy hat, and he tips it forward and back ever so slightly.

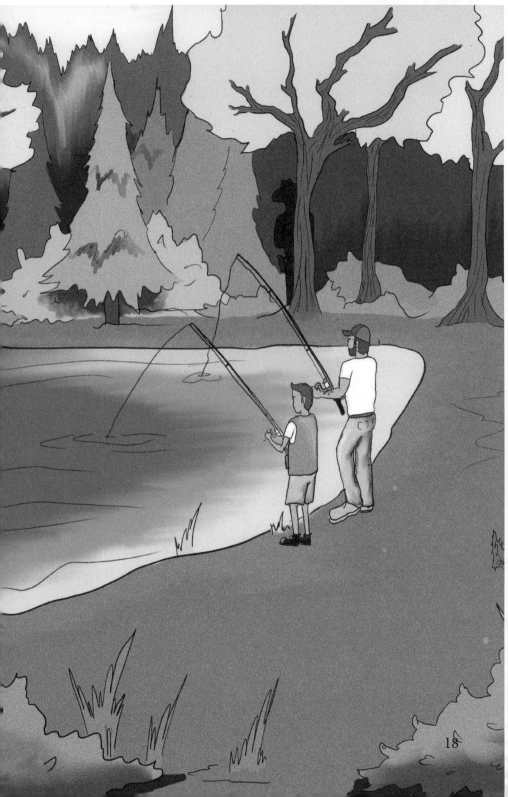

"Hello, fellows. Catching anything?" the man says in a deep booming voice.

Bobby's Dad greets the man in the cow-boy hat. It's then that the two start talking and it seems like they know each other. Bobby doesn't follow much of what they are saying partly because a mosquito keeps buzzing by his ear and partly because Bobby can't keep his eyes off the man's shiny badge.

And just as quickly and secretly as the man arrived, he disappears back into the woods.

"Dad, who was that cowboy in the woods?" Bobby asks his Dad.

His Dad lets out a laugh, "Ha! Cowboy in the woods? Why that was the game warden. Checking to make sure we had a fishing license and not catching too many fish."

They start to pack up their fishing gear. "But where did he come from? Why didn't he come from the trail and the parking lot?" Bobby asks.

"Good questions! Those guys always seem to pop out of the woods. They make sure everyone is following the rules and laws in the woods."

Wow, thinks Bobby, a wildlife police officer! He wonders if the man in the cowboy hat has ever solved a run-over-frog case.

For the next few days, Bobby can't stop thinking about the game warden. He searches his brother and sister's dress-up clothes for a cowboy hat, but the only cowboy-looking hat he finds is way too small and bright red. That just doesn't look professional enough.

On Saturday, Bobby puts on his vest and sets out on a walk in the woods.

Trails in his backyard crisscross with other neighborhood trails. He passes his brother and sister and some other kids.

"Want to help us make a fort?" Jeremy asks as he pushes a large branch into place. They're creating some sort of teepee. Bobby watches for a few minutes, but then continues on his way in search of more clues.

He follows a line of ants.

He watches a bird fly to its nest in a tree.

As Bobby walks closer to Moon Pond, he can hear voices. Bobby remembers how the Cowboy in the Woods was able to stay hidden in the trees and thinks he should try to do that too. He carefully walks off trail, stepping in between sticks and staying hidden behind tree trunks. Closer and closer he creeps until he's close enough to hear and see what's going on.

Four boys are fishing. One of them is Nick Sullivan – a kid one grade higher than Bobby. The other three look just like Nick, but older – probably brothers.

"Do you think we have enough?" Nick asks his older brothers while holding up a line of eight fish.

"Nah, come on, Nick. Keep fishing. We need at least twenty. I bet I can get the most." The boys continue to fish in Moon Pond while Bobby watches from the woods. The Sullivan kids pull fish after fish out of the pond—way too many fish, Bobby thinks. How could anyone eat this much? Would they fish everything out of the pond? Bobby stays hidden and continues to write in his notebook, making a tick mark every time another fish is caught.

After about an hour, the Sullivan kids start packing up. One of the older boys says, "Wow! I think this is our biggest haul yet! We'll make two hundred bucks after we sell it to Mr. Brown! Now, don't forget, Nick. Don't say anything to your friends at school. This fishing trip is a secret." Nick nods in agreement.

"Plus, we don't have a fishing license," laughs the oldest.

Bobby's eyes go wide! His Dad had told him that little kids didn't need a license, but older kids did. He waits for the Sullivan kids to leave, then runs through the woods back to his house.

Bobby finds his Dad in the garage.

"Dad, how old do you have to be again to need a fishing license?" he asks.

"Sixteen, why?" his Dad answers.

"How old does sixteen years look?" Bobby asks.

"What?" His Dad looks confused. Just then a truck pulled into the driveway with the Game Warden driving. He steps out and grabs something from behind his seat.

The Game Warden smiles at Bobby and hands him a small plastic case with flies.

"For the budding fisherman," the Game Warden booms. He ruffles Bobby's hair, like his Aunt Cindy always does, but this time Bobby doesn't mind.

"Thanks," Bobby says, peering into the plastic box. "Um, Mr. Warden. I have a question. How old does sixteen years look?"

"Bobby," his Dad says, "What is this all about?"

Bobby pulls out his notebook and goes over every detail and every bit of evidence. He tells his Dad and the Game Warden about the Sullivan kids, how he knows Nick and how he thinks the others were his older brothers. He tells them how many fish they took and about the comment about not having a license. The Game Warden pulls his own notebook out and copies Bobby's notes down. Then he leaves in a hurry. Bobby's Dad beams proudly at his wildlife detective son.

The next day, the Game Warden comes back and praises Bobby for his detective skills, and presents him with a badge and a hat! Bobby can't believe it himself and spends a lot of time looking in the bathroom mirror at his very own cowboy hat and badge – until his sister bangs on the door 'cause she needs to use the bathroom.'

The word about Bobby gets around. The school newspaper even does a special story about him.

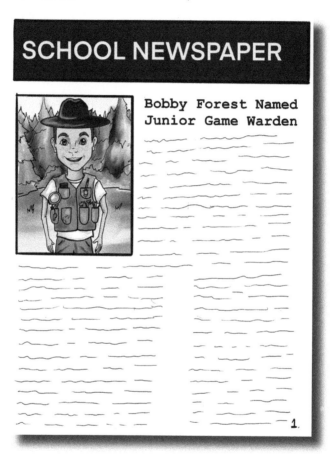

SCHOOL NEWSPAPER

Bobby Forest Named
Junior Game Warden

Bobby spends the whole summer observing wildlife, writing notes in his notebook, fishing with his Dad, and keeping track of all the animals in his neighborhood.

34

It isn't until late summer when he finally sees the Sullivan kids back at Moon Pond. Bobby, hiding in the woods, watches the brothers sitting by the pond's edge, after they went swimming. Bobby wonders if the water felt nice and cool, since he's sweating under his vest and hat. Luckily it starts to rain, instantly cooling down the hot air.

"Come on, guys, let's get out of here," one of the brothers says. "Let's go get ice cream, and play frogger."

"I love that game!" shouts another brother.

"Wait!" Nick says. "Can we get in trouble
for it?"

"Nah, you can't get in trouble for acciden-
tally running over a frog in the road," one
brother replies.

"I wouldn't have hit the frog it you hadn't
distracted me!" laughs another.

Bobby realizes what he's just heard—a
confession! His cowboy style hat keeps
the rain out of his wide-eyed smiling face.
Bobby flips open his notebook and finds
his notes from Mr. Frogger's unsolved
case to write: Case Closed.

Wayne Saunders is a retired Lieutenant Conservation Officer from the New Hampshire Fish and Game Department. An honored and celebrated wildlife Law Enforcement Officer overseeing patrols in the northern reaches of New Hampshire from Mount Washington to the Canadian border, The Cowboy in the Woods was a term he used as a six-year-old hunter to describe his first interaction with a Game Warden. He still considers natural resource protection and education a passion and calling. He currently hosts the popular Podcast Wardens Watch.

Lindsay Webb is a naturalist, wildlife biologist, and environmental educator. She enjoys spending time outdoors with her friends and family, and sharing her stories with others. On any given day, you might find her photographing butterflies, spying on moose, or playing wildlife detective. She's always up for an outdoor adventure!

Ashley Mayers is a wildlife artist who grew up on the beaches of southern New Jersey. She specializes in nautical art and pelagic fish species, and her true passion lies in anything involving the ocean. She is the artist and co-owner of Salt of the Earth, LLC, which is a clothing company focusing on life outdoors. In her down time she enjoys being out on the water, whether it be fishing, surfing, boating or diving.

CPSIA information can be obtained
at www.ICGtesting.com
Printed in the USA
BVHW020450090621
609067BV00001B/1